ELSIE PIDDOCK
SKIPS IN HER SLEEP

ELEANOR FARJEON

ILLUSTRATED BY CHARLOTTE VOAKE

Text copyright © 1937, 1997, 2000 by Gervase Farjeon. Illustrations copyright © 2000 by Charlotte Voake. All rights reserved. First U.S. edition 2000.
ISBN 0-7636-0790-8 Library of Congress Cataloging-in-Publication Data is available. Library of Congress Catalog Card Number 99-053693.
1 2 3 4 5 6 7 8 9 10 Printed in Hong Kong. This book was typeset in Stempel Schneidler Light. The illustrations were done in watercolor and ink.
Candlewick Press, 2067 Massachusetts Avenue, Cambridge, Massachusetts 02140

FOR
SEBASTIAN
WALKER
C.V.

CANDLEWICK PRESS
CAMBRIDGE, MASSACHUSETTS

Elsie Piddock

lived in Glynde under Caburn, where lots of other little girls lived too. They lived mostly on bread-and-butter, because their mothers were too poor to buy cake. As soon as Elsie began to hear, she heard the other little girls skipping every evening after school in the lane outside her mother's cottage. *Swish-swish!* went the rope through the air. *Tappity-tap!* went the little girls' feet on the ground. *Mumble-umble-umble!* went the children's voices, saying a rhyme that the skipper could skip to.

In course of time, Elsie not only heard the sounds, but understood what they were all about, and then the mumble-umble turned itself into words like this:

ANdy SPANdy SUGARdy CANdy,
FRENCH ALmond ROCK!
Breadandbutterforyoursupper's-
allyourmother's-
GOT!

The second bit went twice as fast as the first bit, and when the little girls said it Elsie Piddock, munching her supper, always munched her mouthful of bread-and-butter in double-quick time. She wished she had some Sugardy-Candy-French-Almond-Rock to suck during the first bit, but she never had.

When Elsie Piddock was three years old, she asked her mother for a skipping-rope.

"You're too little," said her mother. "Bide a bit till you're a bigger girl, then you shall have one."

Elsie pouted, and said no more. But in the middle of the night her parents were wakened by something going *Slap-slap!* on the floor, and there was Elsie in her nightgown skipping with her father's braces. She skipped till her feet caught in the tail of them, and she tumbled down and cried. But she had skipped ten times running first.

"Bless my buttons, mother!" said Mr. Piddock. "The child's a born skipper."

And Mrs. Piddock jumped out of bed full of pride, rubbed Elsie's elbows for her, and said: "There-a-there now! Dry your tears, and tomorrow you shall have a skip-rope all of your own."

So Elsie dried her eyes on the hem of her nightgown; and in the morning, before he went to work, Mr. Piddock got a little cord, just the right length, and made two little wooden handles to go on the ends. With this Elsie skipped all day, scarcely stopping to eat her breakfast of bread-and-butter, and her dinner of butter-and-bread.

And in the evening, when the schoolchildren were gathered in the lane, Elsie went out among them, and began to skip with the best.

"Oh!" cried Joan Challon, who was the champion skipper of them all, "just look at little Elsie Piddock skipping as never so!"

All the skippers stopped to look, and then to wonder. Elsie Piddock certainly *did* skip as never so, and they called to their mothers to come and see. And the mothers in the lane came to their doors, and threw up their hands, and cried: "Little Elsie Piddock is a born skipper!"

By the time she was five she could outskip any of them: whether in "Andy-Spandy," "Lady, Lady, Drop your Purse," "Charley Parley Stole some Barley," or whichever of the games it might be. By the time she was six her name and fame were known to all the villages in the county. And by the time she was seven, the fairies heard of her.

They were fond
of skipping themselves,
and they had a special
Skipping-Master who
taught them new skips
every month at the
new moon. As they
skipped they chanted:

The High Skip,
The Sly Skip,
The Skip Like a Feather,
The Long Skip,
The Strong Skip,
And the Skip All Together!
The Slow Skip,
The Toe Skip
The Skip Double-Double,
The Fast Skip,
The Last Skip,
And the Skip Against Trouble!

All these skips
had their own meanings,
and were made up by the
Skipping-Master, whose
name was Andy-Spandy.
He was very proud of his fairies,
because they skipped better than
the fairies of any other county;
but he was also very severe with
them if they did not please him.
    One night he scolded Fairy
Heels-o'-Lead for skipping badly,
and praised Fairy Flea-Foot
for skipping well. Then
    Fairy Heels-o'-Lead sniffed
        and snuffed, and said:

"Hhm-hhm-hhm!
There's a little girl in Glynde
who could skip Flea-Foot
round the moon and
back again. A born skipper
she is, and she skips as never so."
    "What is her name?"
asked Andy-Spandy.
    "Her name is Elsie Piddock,
and she has skipped down
every village far and near,
from Didling to Wannock."
    "Go and fetch her here!"
        commanded
        Andy-Spandy.

Off went Heels-o'-Lead, and poked her head through Elsie's little window under the eaves, crying: "Elsie Piddock! Elsie Piddock! there's a Skipping Match on Caburn, and Fairy Flea-Foot says she can skip better than you."

Elsie Piddock was fast asleep, but the words got into her dream, so she hopped out of bed with her eyes closed, took her skipping-rope, and followed Heels-o'-Lead to the top of Mount Caburn, where Andy-Spandy and the fairies were waiting for them.

"Skip, Elsie Piddock!"

said Andy-Spandy, "and show us what you're worth!"

Elsie twirled her rope and skipped in her sleep, and as she skipped she murmured:

ANdy SPANdy SUGARdy CANdy,
FRENCH ALmond ROCK!
Breadandbutterforyoursupper's-
allyourmother's-
GOT!

Andy-Spandy watched her skipping with his eyes as sharp as needles, but he could find no fault with it, nor could the fairies.

"Very good, as far as it goes!" said Andy-Spandy. "Now let us see how far it *does* go. Stand forth, Elsie and Flea-Foot, for the Long Skip."

Elsie had never done the Long Skip, and if she had had all her wits about her she wouldn't have known what

Andy-Spandy meant; but as she was dreaming, she understood him perfectly. So she twirled her rope, and as it came over jumped as far along the ground as she could, about twelve feet from where she had started. Then Flea-Foot did the Long Skip, and skipped clean out of sight.

"Hum!" said Andy-Spandy. "Now, Elsie Piddock, let us see you do the Strong Skip."

Once more Elsie understood what was wanted of her; she put both feet together, jumped her rope, and came down with all her strength, so that her heels sank into the ground. Then Flea-Foot did the Strong Skip, and sank into the ground as deep as her waist.

"Hum!" said Andy-Spandy. "And now, Elsie Piddock, let us see you do the Skip All Together."

At his words, all the fairies leaped to their ropes, and began skipping as lively as they could, and Elsie with them. An hour went by, two hours, and three hours; one by one the fairies fell down exhausted, and Elsie Piddock skipped on. Just before morning she was skipping all by herself.

Then Andy-Spandy wagged his head and said: "Elsie Piddock, you are a born skipper. There's no tiring you at all. And for that you shall come once a month to Caburn when the moon is new, and I will teach you to skip till a year is up. And after that I'll wager there won't be mortal or fairy to touch you."

Andy-Spandy was as good
as his word. Twelve times during
the next year Elsie Piddock rose
up in her sleep with the new
moon, and went to the top of
Mount Caburn. There she took
her place among the fairies, and
learned to do all the tricks of
the skipping-rope, until she
did them better than any.
At the end of the
year she did the
High Skip so
well, that she
skipped right
over the
moon.

In the Sly Skip not
a fairy could catch her,
or know where she would
skip to next; so artful was
she, that she could
skip through the
lattice of a skeleton
leaf, and never
break it.

She redoubled the Skip
Double-Double, in which you only
had to double yourself up twice
round the skipping-rope before
it came down.
Elsie Piddock did
it four times.

In the Fast Skip, she skipped
so fast that you couldn't see her,
though she stood on the same
spot all the time.

In the Slow Skip, she skipped
so slow that a mole had time to
throw up his hill under her rope
before she came down.

In the Toe Skip, when all the
others skipped on their tip-toes,
Elsie never touched a grass-blade
with more than the edge
of her toe-nail.

In the Last Skip, when all the
fairies skipped over the same rope
in turn, running round and round
till they made a mistake from
giddiness, Elsie never got giddy,
and never made a mistake, and
was always left in last.

In the Skip Against Trouble,
she skipped so joyously that
Andy-Spandy himself
chuckled with delight.

In the Long Skip
she skipped
from Caburn
to the other end
of Sussex, and had to be
fetched back by the wind.

In the Strong Skip,
she went right under the
earth, as a diver goes under
the sea, and the rabbits,
whose burrows she had
disturbed, handed
her up again.

But in the
Skip like a Feather
she came down like gossamer,
so that she could alight on
a spider-thread and never shake
the dew-drop off.

And in the Skip All Together,
she could skip down the
whole tribe of fairies,
and remain as fresh
as a daisy. Nobody
had ever found
out how long
Elsie Piddock
could skip without
getting tired, for everybody else got
tired first. Even Andy-Spandy
didn't know.

At the end of the year he said
to her: "Elsie Piddock, I have taught

you all. Bring me your skipping-rope, and you shall have a prize."

Elsie gave her rope to Andy-Spandy, and he licked the two little wooden handles, first the one and then the other. When he handed the rope back to her, one of the handles was made of Sugar Candy, and the other of French Almond Rock.

"There!" said Andy-Spandy. "Though you suck them never so, they will never grow less, and you shall therefore suck sweet all your life. And as long as you are little enough to skip with this rope, you shall skip as I have taught you. But when you are too big for this rope, and must get a new one, you will no longer be able to do all the fairy skips that you have learned, although you will still skip better in the mortal way than any other girl that ever was born. Good-bye, Elsie Piddock."

"Aren't I ever going to skip for you again?" asked Elsie Piddock in her sleep.

But Andy-Spandy didn't answer. For morning had come over the Downs, and the fairies disappeared, and Elsie Piddock went back to bed.

If Elsie had been famous for her skipping before this fairy year, you can imagine what she became after it. She created so much wonder, that she hardly dared to show all she could do.

Nevertheless, for another year she did such incredible things, that people came from far and near to see her skip over the church spire, or through the split oak-tree in the Lord's Park, or across the river at its widest point.

When there was trouble in her mother's house, or in any house in the village, Elsie Piddock skipped so gaily that the trouble was forgotten in laughter.

And when she skipped all the old games in Glynde, along with the little girls, and they sang:

ANdy SPANdy SUGARdy CANdy,
FRENCH ALmond ROCK!
Breadandbutterforyoursupper's-
allyourmother's-
GOT!

Elsie Piddock said: "It aren't all *I've* got!" and gave them a suck of her skipping-rope handles all round. And on the night of the new moon, she always led the children up Mount Caburn, where she skipped more marvellously than ever.

In fact, it was Elsie Piddock who established the custom of New-Moon-Skipping on Caburn.

But at the end of another year she had grown too big to skip with her little rope. She laid it away in a box, and went on skipping with a longer one. She still skipped as never so, but her fairy tricks were laid by with the rope, and though her friends teased her to do the marvellous things she used to do, Elsie Piddock only laughed, and shook her head, and never told why. In time, when she was still the pride and wonder of her village, people would say: "Ah, but you should ha' seen her when she was a littling! Why, she could skip through her mother's keyhole!" And in more time, these stories became a legend that nobody believed. And in still more time, Elsie grew up (though never very much), and became a little woman, and gave up skipping, because skipping-time was over. After fifty years or so, nobody remembered that she had ever skipped at all. Only Elsie knew. For when times were hard, and they often were, she sat by the hearth with her dry crust and no butter, and sucked the Sugar Candy that Andy-Spandy had given her for life.

It was ever and ever so long afterwards. Three new Lords had walked in the Park since the day when Elsie Piddock had skipped through the split oak. Changes had come in the village; old families had died out, new families had arrived; others had moved away to distant parts, the Piddocks among them. Farms had changed hands, cottages had been pulled down, and new ones had been built. But Mount Caburn was as it always had been, and as the people came to think it always would be. And still the children kept the custom of going there each new moon to skip. Nobody remembered how this custom had come about, it was too far back in the years. But customs are customs, and the child who could not skip the new moon in on Caburn stayed at home and cried.

Then a new Lord came to the Park; one not born a Lord, who had grown rich in trade, and bought the old estate. Soon after his coming, changes began to take place more violent than the pulling down of cottages. The new Lord began to shut up footpaths and destroy rights of way. He stole the Common rights here and there, as he could. In his greed for more than he had got, he raised rents and pressed the people harder than they could bear. But bad as the high rents were to them, they did not mind these so much as the loss of their old rights. They fought the new Lord, trying to keep what had been theirs for centuries, and sometimes they won the fight, but oftener lost it. The constant quarrels bred a spirit of anger between them and the Lord, and out of hate he was prepared to do whatever he could to spite them.

Amongst the lands over which he exercised a certain power was Caburn. This had been always open to the people, and the Lord determined if he could to close it. Looking up the old deeds, he discovered that, though the Down was his, he was obliged to leave a way upon it by which the people could go from one village to another. For hundreds of years they had made a short cut of it over the top.

The Lord's Lawyer told him that, by the wording of the deeds, he could never stop the people from travelling by way of the Downs.

"Can't I!" snorted the Lord. "Then at least I will make them travel a long way round!"

And he had plans drawn up to enclose the whole of the top of Caburn, so that nobody could walk on it. This meant that the people must trudge miles round the base, as they passed from place to place.

The Lord gave out that he needed Mount Caburn to build great factories on.

The village was up in arms to defend its rights.

"Can he do it?" they asked those who knew; and they were told: "It is not quite certain, but we fear he can." The Lord himself was not quite certain either but he went on with his plans, and each new move was watched with anger and anxiety by the villagers. And not only by the villagers; for the fairies saw that their own skipping-ground was threatened. How could they ever skip there again when the grass was turned to cinders, and the new moon blackened by chimney-smoke?

The Lawyer said to the Lord: "The people will fight you tooth and nail."

"Let 'em!" blustered the Lord; and he asked uneasily: "Have they a leg to stand on?"

"Just half a leg," said the Lawyer. "It would be as well not to begin building yet, and if you can come to terms with them you'd better."

The Lord sent word
to the villagers that, though
he undoubtedly could do what he
pleased, he would, out of his good
heart, restore to them a footpath
he had blocked, if they would
give up all pretensions to Caburn.

"Footpath, indeed!" cried stout
John Maltman, among his cronies
at the Inn. "What's a footpath to
Caburn? Why, our mothers skipped
there as children, and our children
skip there now. And we hope to see
our children's children skip there.
If Caburn top be built over, 'twill
fair break my little Ellen's heart."

"Ay, and my Margery's,"
said another.

"And my Mary's and Kitty's!"
cried a third. Others spoke up,
for nearly all had daughters
whose joy it was to skip on
Caburn at the new moon.

John Maltman turned to their
best adviser, who had studied the
matter closely, and asked: "What think
ye? Have we a leg to stand on?"

"Only half a one," said the other.
"I doubt if you can stop him. It
might be as well to come to terms."

"None of his footpaths for us,"
swore stout John Maltman. "We'll
fight the matter out."

So things were left for a little, and
each side wondered what the next
move would be. Only the people
knew in their hearts that they must be
beaten in the end and the Lord was
sure of his victory. So sure, that
he had great loads of bricks
ordered; but he did not
begin building for fear the
people might grow violent,
and perhaps burn his ricks
and destroy his property.

The only thing he did was
to put a wire fence round the top
of Caburn, and set a keeper there
to send the people round it.

The people broke the fence in many
places, and jumped it, and crawled
under it; and as the keeper could
not be everywhere at once, many
of them crossed the Down almost
under his nose.

KEEP
OUT

One evening, just before the new moon was due, Ellen Maltman went into the woods to cry. For she was the best skipper under Mount Caburn, and the thought that she would never skip there again made her more unhappy than she had ever thought she could be. While she was crying in the dark, she felt a hand on her shoulder, and a voice said to her: "Crying for trouble, my dear? That'll never do!"

The voice might have been the voice of a withered leaf, it was so light and dry; but it was also kind, so Ellen checked her sobs and said: "It's a big trouble, ma'am, there's no remedy against it *but* to cry."

"Why, yes, there is," said the withered voice. "Ye should skip against trouble, my dear."

At this Ellen's sobs burst forth anew. "I'll never skip no more!" she wailed. "If I can't skip the new moon in on Caburn, I'll never skip no more."

"And why can't you skip the new moon in on Caburn?" asked the voice.

Then Ellen told her. After a little pause the voice spoke quietly out of the darkness. "It's more than you will break their hearts if they cannot skip on Caburn. And it must not be, it must not be. Tell me your name."

"Ellen Maltman, ma'am, and I do love skipping. I can skip down anybody, ma'am, and they say I skip as never so!"

"They do, do they?" said the withered voice. "Well, Ellen, run you home and tell them this. They are to go to this Lord and tell him he shall have his way and build on Caburn, if he will first take down the fence and let all who have ever skipped there skip there once more by turns, at the new moon. *All*, mind you, Ellen. And when the last skipper skips the last skip, he may lay his first brick. And let it be written out on paper, and signed and sealed."

"But ma'am!"
said Ellen, wondering.

"No words, child. Do as I tell you." And the withered voice sounded so compelling that Ellen resisted no more. She ran straight to the village, and told her story to everybody.

At first they could hardly swallow it; and even when they had swallowed it, they said: "But what's the sense of it?" But Ellen persisted and persisted; something of the spirit of the old voice got into her words, and against their reason the people began to think it was the thing to do.

To cut a long story short they sent the message to the Lord next day.

The Lord could scarcely believe his ears. He rubbed his hands, and chortled at the people for fools.

"They've come to terms!" he sneered. "I shall have the Down, and keep my footpath too. Well, they shall have their Skipping-Party; and the moment it is ended, up go my factories!"

The paper was drawn out, signed by both parties in the presence of witnesses, and duly sealed; and on the night of the new moon, the Lord invited a party of his friends to go with him to Caburn to see the sight.

And what a sight it was for
them to see; every little girl
in the village was there with her
skipping-rope, from the toddlers
to those who had just turned
up their hair. Nay, even the grown
maidens and the young mothers
were there; and the very matrons
too had come with ropes.
Had not they once as children
skipped on Caburn? And the
message had said "All."
Yes, and others were there,
others they could not see:

Andy-Spandy and his
fairy team, Heels-o'-Lead,
Flea-Foot, and all of the
rest, were gathered round
to watch with bright
fierce eyes the last
great skipping on
their precious ground.

The skipping began. The toddlers first, a skip or so apiece, a stumble, and they fell out. The Lord and his party laughed aloud at the comical mites, and at another time the villagers would have laughed too. But there was no laughter in them tonight. Their eyes were bright and fierce like those of the fairies. After the toddlers the little girls skipped in the order of their ages, and as they got older, the skipping got better. In the thick of the schoolchildren, "This will take some time," said the Lord impatiently.

And when Ellen Maltman's turn came, and she went into her thousands, he grew restive. But even she, who could skip as never so, tired at last; her foot tripped, and she fell on the ground with a little sob. None lasted even half her time; of those who followed some were better, some were worse, than others; and in the small hours the older women were beginning to take their turn.

Few of them kept it up for half a minute; they hopped and puffed bravely, but their skipping days were done. As they had laughed at the babies, so now the Lord's friends jibed at the babies' grandmothers.

"Soon over now," said the Lord, as the oldest of the women who had come to skip, a fat old dame of sixty-seven, stepped out and twirled her rope.

Her foot caught in it; she staggered, dropped the rope, and hid her face in her hands.

"Done!" shouted the Lord; and he brandished at the crowd a trowel and a brick which he had brought with him. "Clear out, the lot of you! I am going to lay the first brick. The skipping's ended!"

"No, if you please," said a gentle withered voice, "it is *my* turn now." And out of the crowd stepped a tiny tiny woman, so very old, so very bent and fragile, that she seemed to be no bigger than a little child.

"You!" cried the Lord. "Who are *you*?"

"My name is Elsie Piddock, if you please, and I am a hundred and nine years old. For the last seventy-nine years I have lived over the border, but I was born in Glynde, and I skipped on Caburn as a child." She spoke like one in a dream, and her eyes were closed.

"Elsie Piddock! Elsie Piddock!" the name ran in a whisper round the crowd.

"Elsie Piddock!" murmured Ellen Maltman. "Why, Mum, I thought Elsie Piddock was just a tale."

"Nay, Elsie Piddock was no tale!" said the fat woman who had skipped last. "My mother Joan skipped with her many a time, and told me tales you never would believe."

"Elsie Piddock!" they all breathed again; and a wind seemed to fly round Mount Caburn, shrilling the name with glee. But it was no wind, it was Andy-Spandy and his fairy team, for they had seen the skipping-rope in the tiny woman's hands.

One of the handles was made of Sugar Candy, and the other was made of French Almond Rock.

But the new Lord had never even heard of Elsie Piddock as a story; so laughing coarsely once again, he said: "One more bump for an old woman's bones! Skip, Elsie Piddock, and show us what you're worth."

"Yes, skip, Elsie Piddock," cried Andy-Spandy and the fairies, "and show them what you're worth!"

Then Elsie Piddock stepped into the middle of the onlookers, twirled her baby rope over her little shrunken body, and began to skip. And she skipped as NEVER so!

First of all she skipped:

ANdy SPANdy SUGARdy CANdy,
FRENCH ALmond ROCK!
Breadandbutterforyoursupper's-
allyourmother's-
GOT!

And nobody
could find fault with her
skipping. Even the Lord gasped:
"Wonderful! Wonderful for an old
woman!" But Ellen Maltman, who
knew, whispered: "Oh, Mum! 'tis

wonderful for *any*body! And
oh Mum, do but see—she's
skipping in her sleep!"

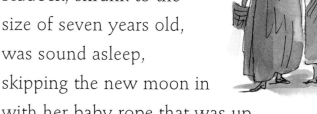

It was true. Elsie
Piddock, shrunk to the
size of seven years old,
was sound asleep,
skipping the new moon in
with her baby rope that was up
to all the tricks. An hour went by,
two hours, three hours. There was
no stopping her, and no tiring her.
The people gasped, the Lord fumed,
and the fairies turned head-over-
heels for joy. When morning
broke the Lord cried:

"That's enough!"
But Elsie Piddock
went on skipping.
"Time's up!"
cried the Lord.
"When I skip my last
skip, you shall lay your first
brick," said Elsie Piddock.

The villagers broke into a cheer.

"Signed and sealed, my Lord, signed and sealed," said Elsie Piddock.

"But hang it, old woman, you can't go on for ever!" cried the Lord.

"Oh yes, I can," said Elsie Piddock. And on she went.

At midday the Lord shouted: "Will the woman never stop?"

"No, she won't," said Elsie Piddock. And she didn't.

"Then I'll stop you!" stormed the Lord, and made a grab at her.

"Now for a Sly Skip," said Elsie Piddock, and skipped right through his thumb and forefinger.

"Hold her, you!" yelled the Lord to his Lawyer.

"Now for a High Skip," said Elsie Piddock, and as the Lawyer darted at her, she skipped right over the highest lark singing in the sun.

The villagers shouted for glee, and the Lord and his friends were furious. Forgotten was the compact signed and sealed— their one thought now was to seize the maddening old woman, and stop her skipping by sheer force.

But they couldn't.
She played all her
tricks on them:
High Skip,
　　Slow Skip,
　　　Sly Skip,
　　Toe Skip,
　　　Long Skip,
　　　Fast Skip,
Strong Skip,
　　but never
　　　Last Skip.
On and on
and on
she went.

When the sun
began to set, she
was still skipping.
"Can we never
rid the Down of
the old thing?"
cried the Lord
desperately.

"No," answered
Elsie Piddock
in her sleep,
"the Down will never be rid of
me more. It's the children of
Glynde I'm skipping for, to hold
the Down for them and theirs
for ever; it's Andy-Spandy
I'm skipping for once again,
for through him I've
sucked sweet
all my life.

Oh, Andy, even you never
knew how long Elsie Piddock
could go on skipping!"

"The woman's mad!"
cried the Lord. "Signed and sealed
doesn't hold with a madwoman.
Skip or no skip, I shall lay
the first brick!"

He plunged his trowel into
the ground, and forced his
brick down into the hole
as a token of his
possession of the land.

"Now," said Elsie
Piddock, "for a Strong Skip!"

Right on the top
of the brick she skipped,
and down underground
she sank out of sight,

bearing the brick
beneath her. Wild with rage,
the Lord dived after her.
Up came Elsie Piddock
skipping blither than ever—
but the Lord never came up
again. The Lawyer ran to
look down the hole; but
there was no sign of him.
The Lawyer reached
his arm down the hole;
but there was no
reaching him. The Lawyer
dropped a pebble
down the hole; and no one
heard it fall. So strong
had Elsie Piddock
skipped the
Strong Skip.

The Lawyer shrugged his shoulders, and he and the Lord's friends left Mount Caburn for good and all. Oh, how joyously Elsie Piddock skipped then!

"Skip Against Trouble!" cried she, and skipped so that everyone present burst into happy laughter. To the tune of it she skipped the Long Skip, clean out of sight.

And the people went home
to tea. Caburn was saved
for their children,
and for the fairies,
for ever.

But that wasn't the end
of Elsie Piddock; she has never
stopped skipping on Caburn since,
for Signed and Sealed is Signed
and Sealed. Not many have seen
her, because she knows all the
tricks; but if you go to Caburn at
the new moon, you may catch
a glimpse of a tiny bent figure,
no bigger than a child, skipping
all by itself in its sleep, and hear
a gay little voice, like the voice
of a dancing yellow leaf, singing:

ANdy SPANdy SUGARdy CANdy,
FRENCH ALmond ROCK!
Breadandbutterforyoursupper's-
allyourmother's-
GOT!